Written by Sheila Higginson
Illustrated by the Imaginism Studio
and the Disney Storybook Art Team

Ashland, OH 44805
www.bendonpub.com

This is **VAMPIRINA HAUNTLEY**.
Her family calls her Vee.
You can, too!

Boris and Oxana are Vee's dad and mom.
They are very proud of their little girl!

The Hauntleys are a
little **DIFFERENT** from most families.

Can you guess why?
Connect the dots to see what makes them special.

VEE IS A VAMPIRE!

She lives in Transylvania.
She has lots of **COOL** monster friends there.

© Disney

VAMPIRINA HAUNTLEY

How many words can you make
from the letters in Vampirina Hauntley?

_____   _____

_____   _____

_____   _____

_____   _____

_____   _____

_____

_____

_____

_____

_____

She has other friends, too.
Demi is the **GHOST** who haunts Vee's house.

HOW MANY?

Count the bats. How many do you see?

Your
Answer

MISSING PIECE

Circle the missing piece of the puzzle.

1

2

3

OXANA

Using the grid as a guide, draw the character in the box below.

SHADOW MATCH

Which shadow matches Vee?

A

B

C

Your
Answer

Chef Remy is the family chef who cooks
the **SPOOKIEST** meals in Transylvania!

TRANSYLVANIA

How many words can you make
from the letters in Transylvania?

_____   _____

_____   _____

_____   _____

_____   _____

_____   _____

_____

_____

_____

_____

WHICH ARE THE SAME?

Which two images are the same?

A

B

C

D

Your
Answer

Wolfie is the family pet.

SHADOW MATCH

Which shadow matches Wolfie?

Your
Answer

A

B

C

WHICH ARE THE SAME?

Which two images are the same?

A

B

C   **D**

Your
Answer

Oxana

© Disney

Boris and Oxana have a surprise for Vee.
Use the code to find out what the message says.

The Hauntleys are **MOVING** to Pennsylvania!

© Disney

HOW MANY?

Count the ghosts. How many do you see?

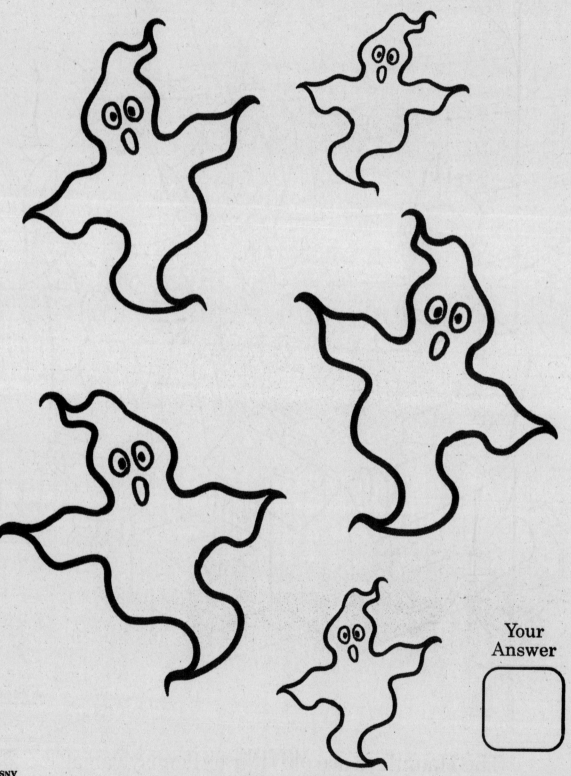

Your
Answer

They're going to live in their Great Uncle Dieter's house.

"It's going to be a family adventure!" Boris tells Vee.

Draw a picture of Vee saying good-bye to her friends.

SHADOW MATCH

Which shadow matches Vee?

A

B

C

Your Answer

HOW MANY?

Count the moons. How many do you see?

Your
Answer

TIC-TAC-TOE

HELLO, PENNSYLVANIA!

"It sure looks **SPOOKY** in here," Vee says.
"It feels like home!"

There are 6 differences between the two pictures of Vee's new bedroom. Can you find them?

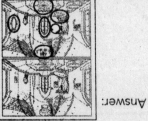

DEMI

Using the grid as a guide,
draw the character in the
box below.

MISSING PIECE

Circle the missing piece of the puzzle.

1

2

3

Vee and Demi play vampire tag in the new house.
"No fair disappearing through things!" Vee shouts.

FOLLOW THE PATH

Which path leads to Boris?

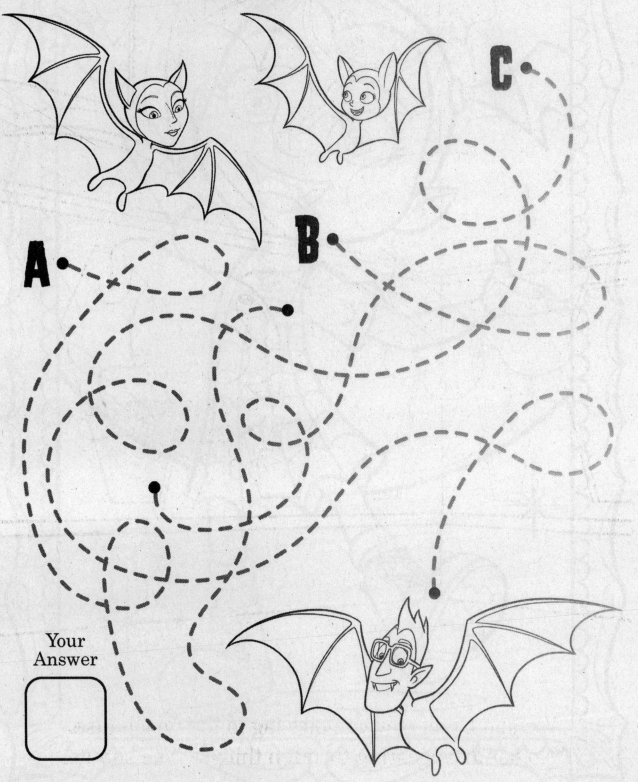

Your Answer

© Disney

TIC-TAC-TOE

SPOOKY SQUARES

Example

Taking turns, connect a line from one dot to another. Whoever makes the line that completes a box puts his or her initial inside the box. The person with the most squares at the end of the game wins!

WHICH ARE THE SAME?

Which two images are the same?

A
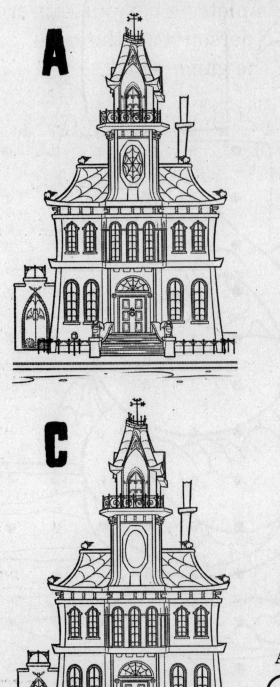

B

C

D
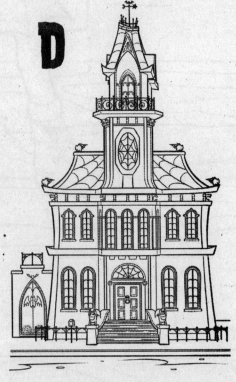

Your
Answer

© Disney

Vee meets Gregoria, the **GRUMPY** gargoyle.
She's lived in the house for hundreds of years!

FOLLOW THE PATH

Which path leads to Gregoria?

A.

B.

C.

Your
Answer

© Disney

FOLLOW THE PATH

Which path leads to Vee?

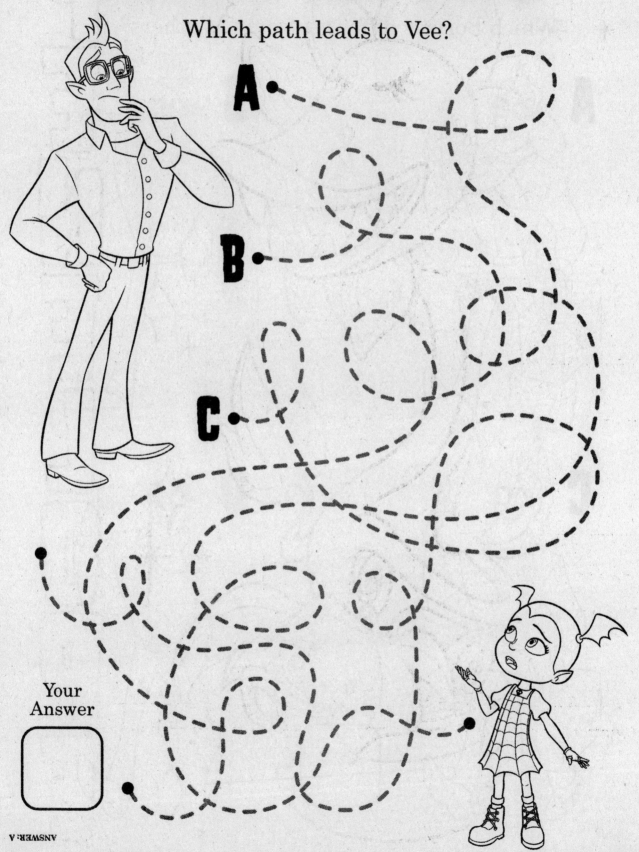

A

B

C

Your Answer

© Disney

WHICH IS DIFFERENT?

Which Boris is different from the others?

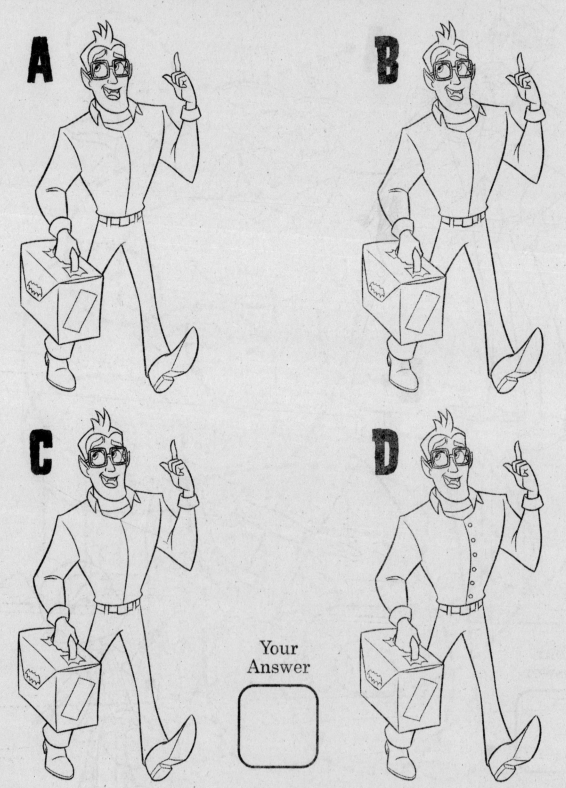

A

B

C

D

Your
Answer

"I can't wait to make more new friends," Vee cheers. "Just remember love," Boris says. "Humans are a little jumpy."

HOW MANY?

Count the vampires. How many do you see?

Your
Answer

MISSING PIECE

Circle the missing piece of the puzzle.

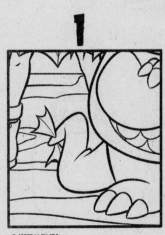

1

2

3

SPOOKY SQUARES

Example

Taking turns, connect a line from one dot to another. Whoever makes the line that completes a box puts his or her initial inside the box. The person with the most squares at the end of the game wins!

© Disney

EEEKS! The doorbell starts to shriek.
The first visitor has arrived!

"WELCOME TO THE NEIGHBORHOOD!"
says Edna Peepleson.

She gives Oxana a bouquet of flowers.

Look down and across to find the flower names listed below.

X	V	P	O	P	P	Y	U	G	Q
L	I	R	N	S	E	Z	T	M	A
I	O	O	B	P	T	A	H	T	W
L	L	S	L	A	U	G	X	J	D
A	E	E	U	N	N	P	C	O	A
C	T	X	E	S	I	J	U	C	I
E	Y	Y	B	Y	A	N	F	I	S
X	Y	W	E	A	T	Y	M	X	Y
A	L	I	L	Y	D	A	B	X	M
O	T	U	L	I	P	Z	N	W	E

DAISY   **BLUEBELL**

ROSE   **LILY**

PETUNIA   **VIOLET**

TULIP   **POPPY**

PANSY   **LILAC**

Answer:

WHICH IS DIFFERENT?

Which Edna is different from the others?

A

B

C

D

Your Answer

© Disney

Edna meets Penelope the man-eating plant.
"AAHHHHH!!!" she screams.

"You're right, Dad," Vee says. "Humans are jumpy."

FOLLOW THE PATH

Which path leads to the spider?

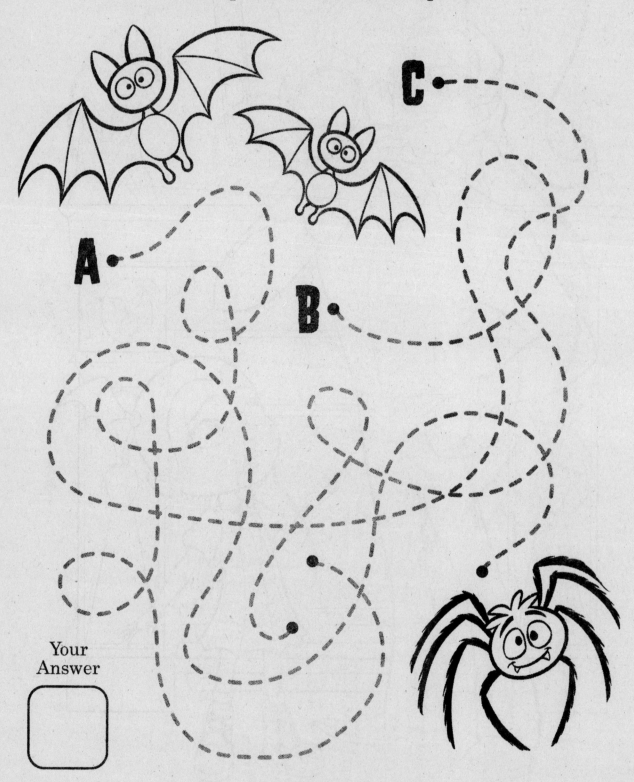

Your
Answer

WOLFIE

© Disney

Draw a picture of your family.

SPOOKY SQUARES

Example

Taking turns, connect a line from one dot to another. Whoever makes the line that completes a box puts his or her initial inside the box. The person with the most squares at the end of the game wins!

SHADOW MATCH

Which shadow matches Boris?

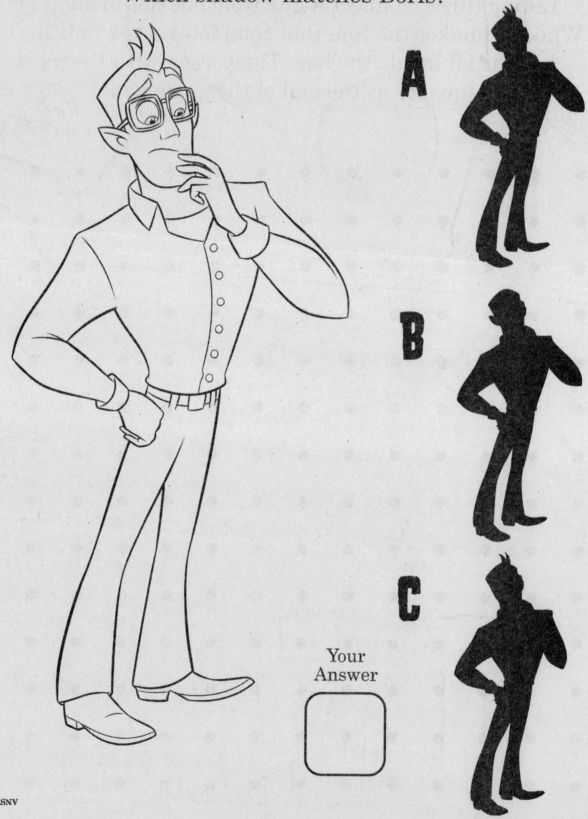

A

B

C

Your
Answer

DEMI

"What if I don't make any friends in Pennsylvania?" she worries.

"Let's show the whole human world how lovable you are!" Demi says.

© Disney

Which picture of Vee and Demi is different?

A

B

C

D

EDNA

Using the grid as a guide, draw the character in the box below.

MISSING PIECE

Circle the missing piece of the puzzle.

1

2

3

"Hi! I'm Poppy," the girl next door says.
"This is my brother Edgar."

"And I'm Bridget!" another girls says.

"I'm Vampirina," says Vee. "I just moved in."

WHICH ARE THE SAME?

Which two images are the same?

A

B

C

Your Answer

D

SHADOW MATCH

Which shadow matches Penelope?

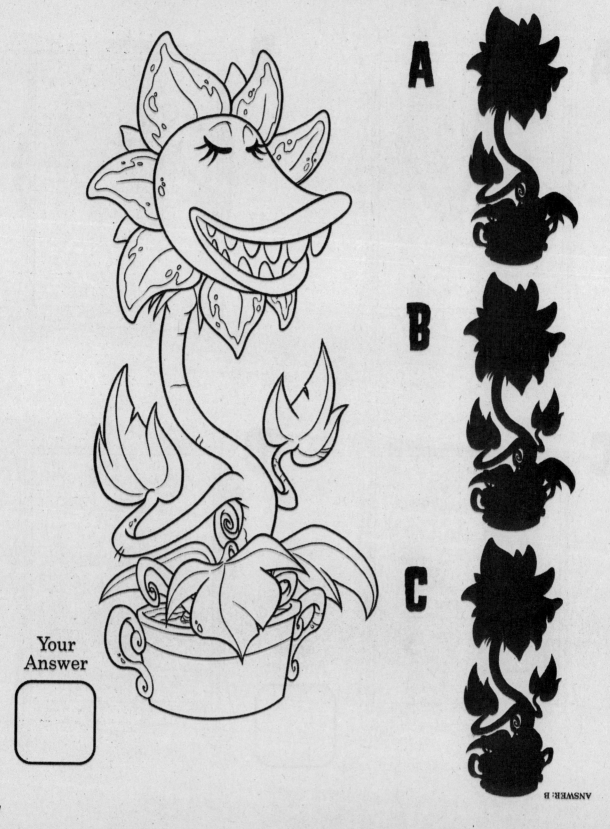

A

B

C

Your Answer

ANSWER: B

WHICH ARE THE SAME?

Which two images are the same?

A

B

C

D

Your
Answer

VEE

HOW MANY?

Count the pumpkins. How many do you see?

Your Answer

"Edgar thinks your house is **HAUNTED**," Poppy admits.

SHADOW MATCH

Which shadow matches Edgar?

A

B

C

Your
Answer

Help Vee lead Poppy and Edgar to her house.

Answer:

"Hello new friends!" Boris and Oxana cheer,
surprising Poppy and Edgar.

"WELCOME!"

HOW MANY?

Count the spiders. How many do you see?

Your
Answer

Vee and Poppy race to Vee's room to play.

© Disney

SHADOW MATCH

Which shadow matches Poppy?

A

B

C

Your
Answer

ANSWER: A

"MEET THE SCREAM GIRL DOLLS!"
Franken-Stacey, Ghastly Gayle and Creepy Caroline.

THE SCREAM GIRL DOLLS

How many words can you make
from the letters in The Scream Girl Dolls?

_____   _____

_____   _____

_____   _____

_____   _____

_____   _____

_____   _____

_____

_____

_____

_____

_____

Can you find 10 bats hidden in this picture?

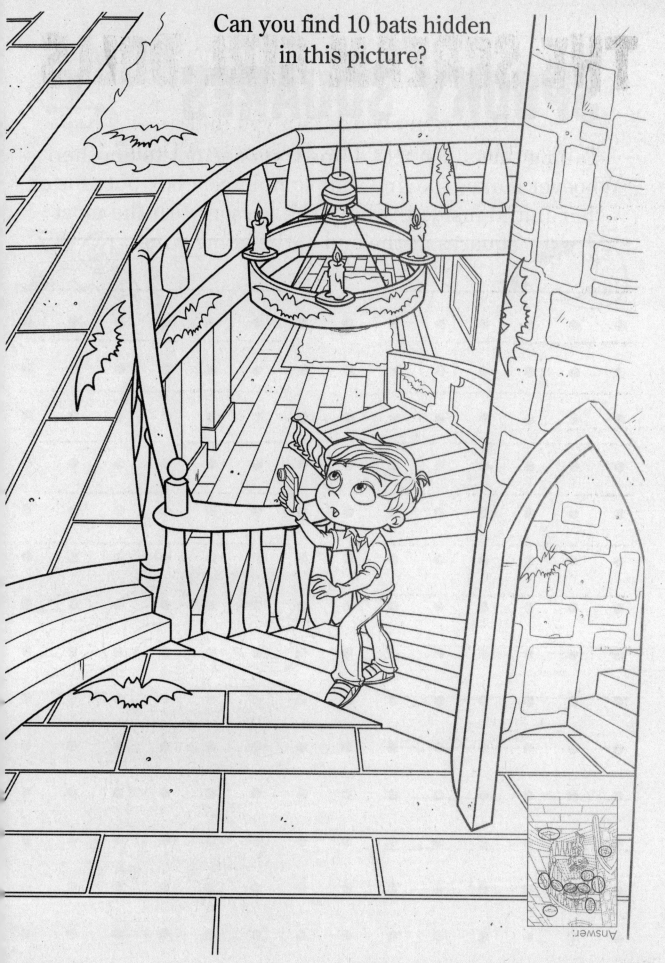

SPOOKY SQUARES

Example

Taking turns, connect a line from one dot to another. Whoever makes the line that completes a box puts his or her initial inside the box. The person with the most squares at the end of the game wins!

EDGAR

Using the grid as a guide, draw the character in the box below.

WHICH ARE THE SAME?

Which two images are the same?

A

B

C

D

Your Answer

GREGORIA

TIC-TAC-TOE

FOLLOW THE PATH

Which path leads to Bridget?

A

B

C

Your
Answer

© Disney

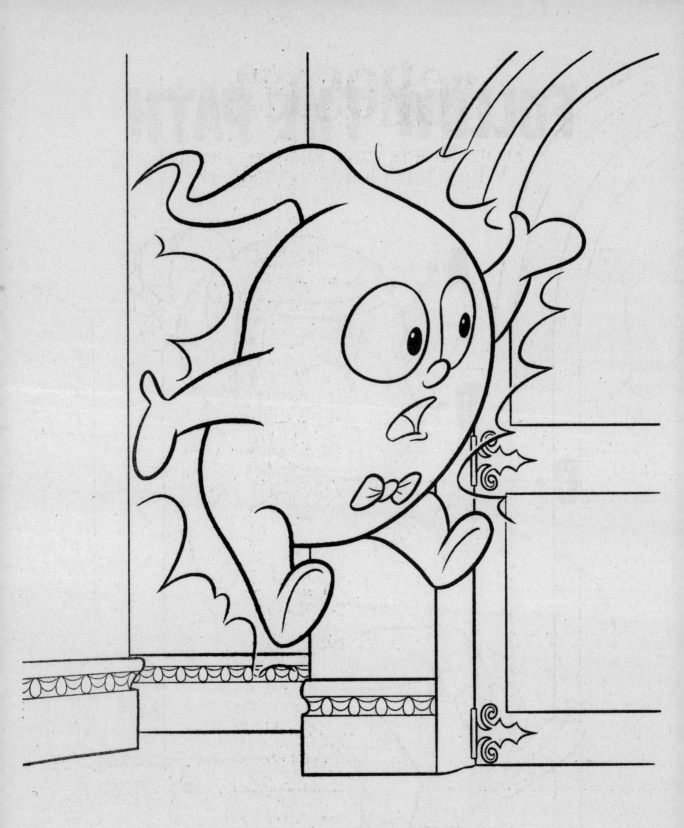

"HUMAN!"

Demi shouts when he sees Poppy.

"GHOST!"

Poppy shouts when she sees Demi.

MISSING PIECE

Circle the missing piece of the puzzle.

1

2

3

MAN-EATING PLANT

How many words can you make
from the letters in Man-Eating Plant?

_____   _____

_____   _____

_____   _____

_____   _____

_____   _____

_____

_____

_____

_____

At the end of each row, circle the correct picture to finish the pattern.

"It's just me, Vampirina," Vee says.

"AH HA!" Edgar says. "I knew something strange was going on in here!"

© Disney

FOLLOW THE PATH

Which path leads to Edgar?

A

B

C

Your
Answer

WORD SEARCH

Look up, down, and across for the words listed below.

V	F	L	S	P	I	D	E	R	S
A	A	S	T	R	A	N	G	E	P
M	O	M	F	I	E	I	N	G	O
P	B	O	P	D	S	G	U	H	O
I	A	A	R	I	J	H	L	O	K
R	T	E	D	E	R	T	D	S	Y
E	S	D	U	T	A	I	E	T	P
S	L	G	M	Z	H	F	N	R	E
Y	C	R	E	E	P	Y	R	A	S
H	A	U	N	T	E	D	N	A	M

BATS   **SPIDERS**
CREEPY   **SPOOKY**
GHOST   **STRANGE**
HAUNTED   **VAMPIRES**
NIGHT   **VAMPIRINA**

"I screamed because we both
love Justin Teether!" Poppy says.

© Disney

"I wanted to be your friend before you turned into a bat," Poppy tells Vee.

"Why wouldn't I want to be
your friend afterwards, too?"

Draw a picture of your favorite toy.

JUSTIN TEETHER

How many words can you make
from the letters in Justin Teether?

_____   _____

_____   _____

_____   _____

_____   _____

_____   _____

_____   _____

_____

_____

_____

_____

WHICH IS DIFFERENT?

Which Edgar is different from the others?

A

B

C

D

Your
Answer

Edna

© Disney

Vee has a new friend, and the Hauntleys are settled in Philadelphia. Now Oxana can open the bed and breakfast she's always dreamed about: the Scare B&B!

Help Vee match the right family portrait to each picture frame.

"Mama, I'll post the Scare B&B online!" Vee says.

WHICH IS DIFFERENT?

Which Vee is different from the others?

Your Answer

SPOOKY SQUARES

Example

Taking turns, connect a line from one dot to another. Whoever makes the line that completes a box puts his or her initial inside the box. The person with the most squares at the end of the game wins!

MISSING PIECE

Circle the missing piece of the puzzle.

1

2

3

Boris has plans for the new house, too.
He invited the Peeplesons to stay for the night!

"What's the worst that could happen!" Oxana wonders.

WHICH IS DIFFERENT?

Which Bridget is different from the others?

A

B

C

D

Your
Answer

TIC-TAC-TOE

Two more guests show up at the front door!
Cosmina and Narcisa are 900-year-old vampire sisters.

Draw a picture of the Hauntley house during the day in the top box. Draw a picture of the Hauntley house at night in the bottom box.

© Disney

HOW MANY?

Count the cauldrons. How many do you see?

Your
Answer

SHADOW MATCH

Which shadow matches Gregoria?

Your
Answer

A   B   C

WHICH IS DIFFERENT?

Which Cosmina is different from the others?

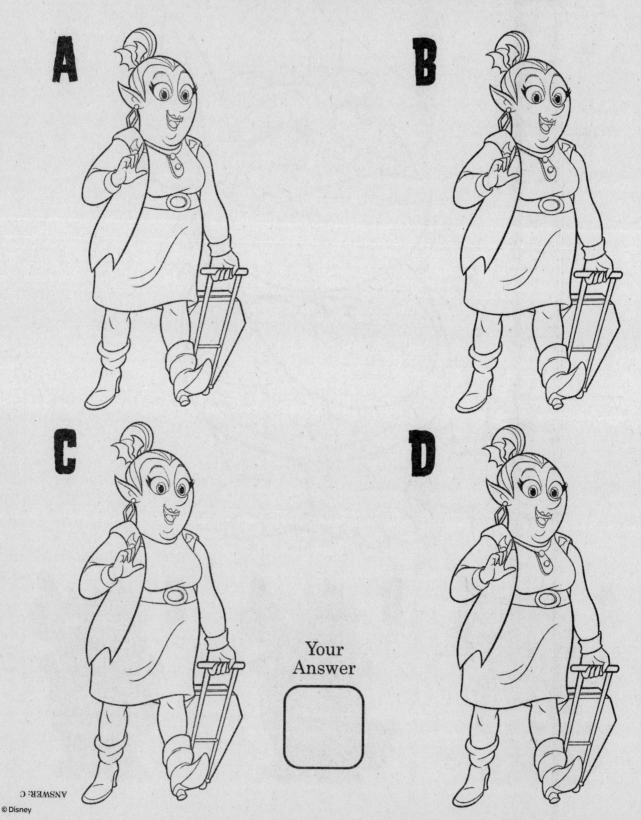

A

B

C

D

Your
Answer

© Disney

"Since vampires sleep during the day and humans sleep at night, they won't need the room at the same time!" Vee says.

VAMPIRINA

Using the grid as a guide, draw the character in the box below.

WHICH ARE THE SAME?

Which two images are the same?

A

B

C

D

Your Answer

Narcisa and Cosmina use the guest room first.
They spread on green frog slime masks before they go to bed.

Oxana makes lunch for the Peeplesons.

Circle all the vegetables you see.

Answer:

TIC-TAC-TOE

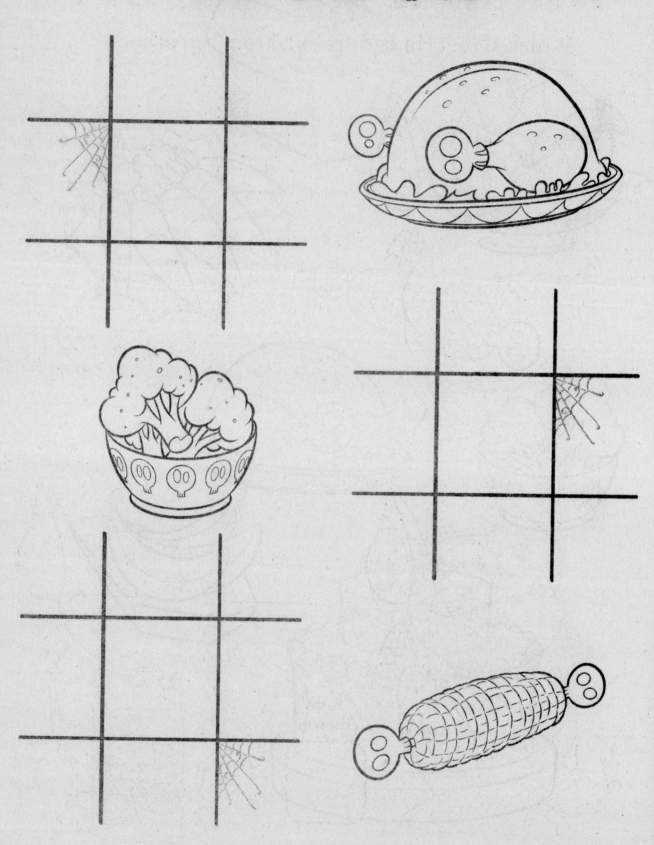

WHICH IS DIFFERENT?

Which Gregoria is different from the others?

A

B

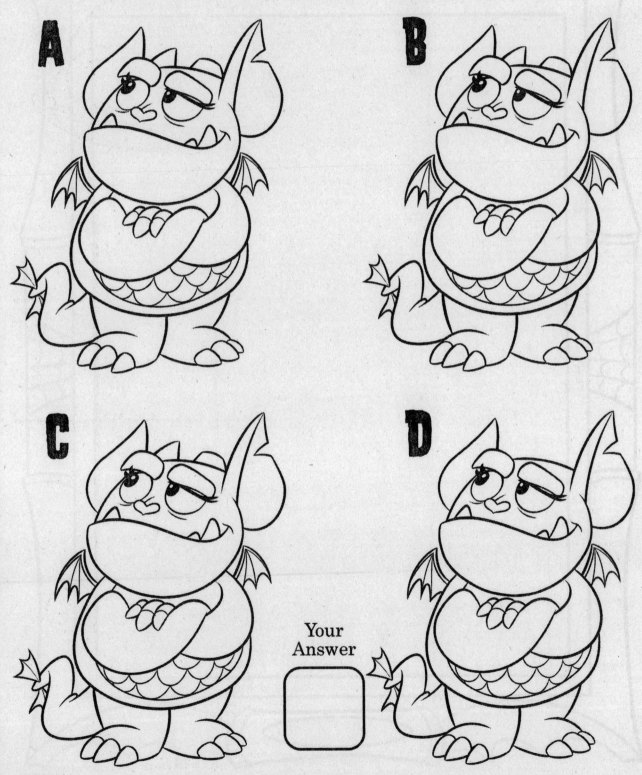

C

D

Your
Answer

ANSWER: D

© Disney

Draw a picture of your favorite food.

GREGORIA

Using the grid as a guide, draw the character in the box below.

VAMPIRE SISTERS

How many words can you make
from the letters in Vampire Sisters?

_____   _____

_____   _____

_____   _____

_____   _____

_____   _____

_____   _____

_____

_____

_____

_____

MISSING PIECE

Circle the missing piece of the puzzle.

1

2

3

TIC-TAC-TOE

© Disney

SPOOKY SQUARES

Example

Taking turns, connect a line from one dot to another. Whoever makes the line that completes a box puts his or her initial inside the box. The person with the most squares at the end of the game wins!

© Disney

When the sun sets, it's time for the Peeplesons to get ready for bed.

That's when Vee wakes the vampire sisters up
and gives them a tour of the neighborhood.

HOW MANY?

Count the webs. How many do you see?

Your
Answer

"Did everything go okay?" Poppy asks when Vee gets back. "Yep!" Vee replies. "But it's a good thing they're leaving in the morning!"

HAUNTED HOUSE

How many words can you make
from the letters in Haunted House?

_____   _____

_____   _____

_____   _____

_____   _____

_____   _____

_____

_____

_____

_____

_____

_____

WHICH IS DIFFERENT?

Which Narcisa is different from the others?

A

B

C

D

Your
Answer

Is that...

...Poppy's mom with Narcisa and Cosmina?
IT IS!

© Disney

All that yoga has made the vampire sisters hungry.
Edna whips up some of her famous blood sausages for them.

FOLLOW THE PATH

Which path leads to Narcisa?

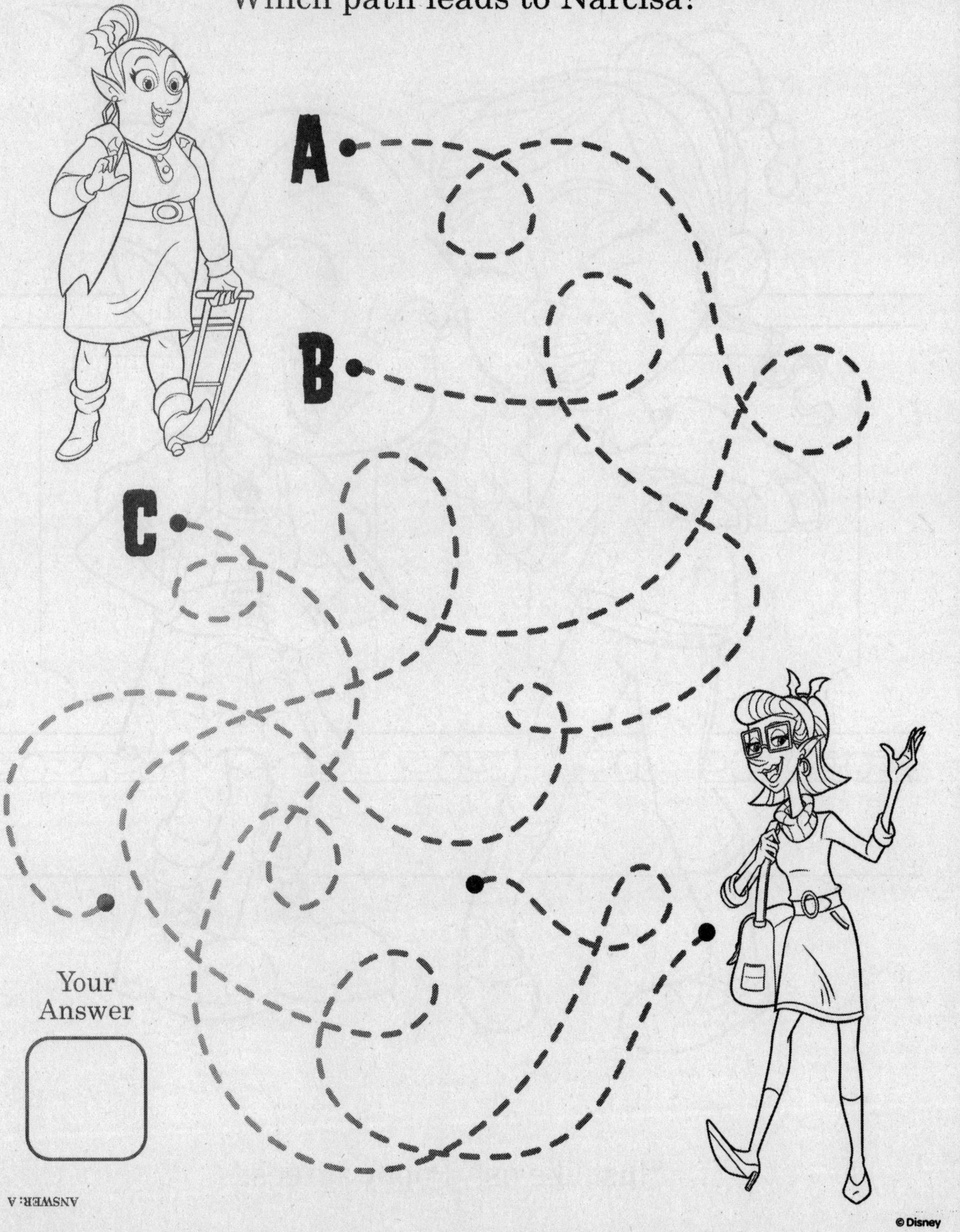

A

B

C

Your
Answer

© Disney

"Looks like your mom and our vampire guests
have a lot in common!" Vee says.

"Just like us!" Poppy agrees.

TIC-TAC-TOE

NARCISSA

COSMINA

WHICH ARE THE SAME?

Which two images are the same?

A

B

C

D

Your
Answer

HOW MANY?

Count the cakes. How many do you see?

Your
Answer

© Disney

Poppy helps Vee get ready for her first day of school!

Vampirina's name starts with the letter V.
Circle four things in the picture that also begin with V.

Vee goes to school with a plant for her new teacher.

POPPY

Using the grid as a guide, draw the character in the box below.

"Come on, Vee!" Poppy calls.

Mr. Gore is Vee's new teacher.

"SMILE!" Mr. Gore says.

"I have an idea!" Poppy says.

Poppy painted a portrait of her best friend!

Vee puts the painting on the class tree. "I think school
in Pennsylvania is going to be just fine," she says.

© Disney

Poppy, Bridget, and Vee are best friends.

Happy Day!

"What shall I wear?"

Daisy is looking lovely.

BLING!

Look up, down, across, and diagonally
for these fun, sparkly blings.

BEADS   **BRACELET**   **NECKLACE**
BELT   **GEM**   **PURSE**
BOWS   **JEWEL**   **RING**

R	✿	B	O	W	S	B	N
I	T	O	J	E	W	E	L
N	⊘	N	A	S	C	A	B
G	E	M	✿	K	I	D	E
W	F	D	L	P	⊘	S	L
B	R	A	C	E	L	E	T
H	C	⊘	V	J	B	✿	A
E	R	B	P	U	R	S	E

© Disney

Minnie loves a bit of bling.
Draw some of your favorite pieces of jewelry.

How sparkly!

"Look at my new ring!"

Minnie is ready to go shopping!.

Daisy

Super cute!

Be happy!

Can you think of five words
that rhyme with **BLING?**
Write (or have someone else write)
the words.

_____

_____

_____

_____

_____

© Disney

Don't be BAAAShful

© Disney

Donald

Butterflies look like bows.

Happy Day!

© Disney

Scooter Girl

Garden Gala

Splish, splash!

Daisy is growing daisies!

More to share!

Help Mickey find Minnie.

Summer blooms!

Draw what Goofy is thinking about.

Minnie

© Disney

Draw what Daisy is thinking about.

What a cutie!

Let's have a
tea party

A purse adds a pop of color.

Minnie and Daisy love to shop!
Draw your favorite dress or outfit.

Help Minnie design the perfect outfit.

Color the dress, purse, and shoes.

Minnie loves her pets!
Draw a picture of your favorite animal.

Figaro

Nose to nose.

Rocker Chick!

Cuckoo-Loca plays for Figaro.

Who Am I?

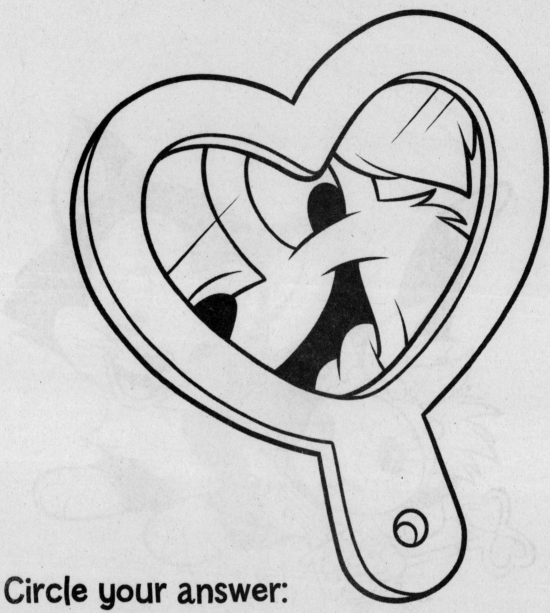

Circle your answer:

Figaro

Clarabelle

Shelby

Cuckoo-Loca

Home Sweet Home

Bath Time

The bubbles are everywhere!

Which one is different?

Shelby

Pluto's Bow

Find and circle 4 differences in the two pictures.

Answers: Minnie's tail is missing, the leash is missing, spots on the dog are missing, Minnie's button is missing.

Lollipop

"A pretty bow for you!"

How sweet!

Looking good!

Animal Friends

How lovely!

A pretty little pet!

Rainy Day

Rainbow!

It's playtime!

Let's take a road trip!

© Disney

Better Together

Connet the dots
to see what Minnie is growing.

Twirly Girl

Tweet-tweet-tweet!

© Disney

So Cute!

Spring Flowers

Find and circle the springtime words.

FLOWER **SPRING**
KITE **RAIN**
RIBBON **RAINBOW**

K	L	R	I	B	B	O	N	I
I	E	O	E	G	R	P	S	
T	Y	H	Z	Q	A	H	F	
E	S	P	R	I	N	G	L	
T	S	T	A	C	I	G	O	
S	R	A	I	N	B	O	W	
B	J	E	N	K	T	A	E	
A	G	T	N	O	W	B	R	

Goofy

Which piece completes the picture?

A   B   C

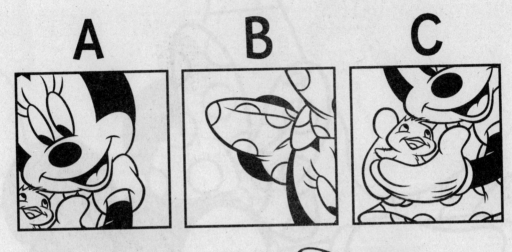

Your
Answer:

Sweet as Springtime!

Sweet as Springtime!

Picture Perfect

Better Together

Make a list of things you love.

I Love . . .

_____

_____

_____

_____

_____

_____

_____

_____

© Disney

A bicycle built for two!

Happy Day!

Hello, little butterfly.

Count each object.
How many are in each group?
Match the number to the
correct number of objects.

1

2

3

4

5

Draw some yummy picnic foods!

Fresh fruit from the garden!

© Disney

Daisy likes cupcakes.

Decorate the cupcake!

© Disney

What a surprise!

Help Minnie, Melody, and Millie get to the picnic table.

Start

Finish

Summer Picnic

Sweet Treat!

A wonderful day for friends to play.

Ready to soar!

Such pretty kites!

Draw a new kite for Minnie.

"What a beautiful day!"

kites
are flowers in the
sky

© Disney

Breezy Day

"A pretty bow for me!"

Use the grid to draw Minnie Mouse.

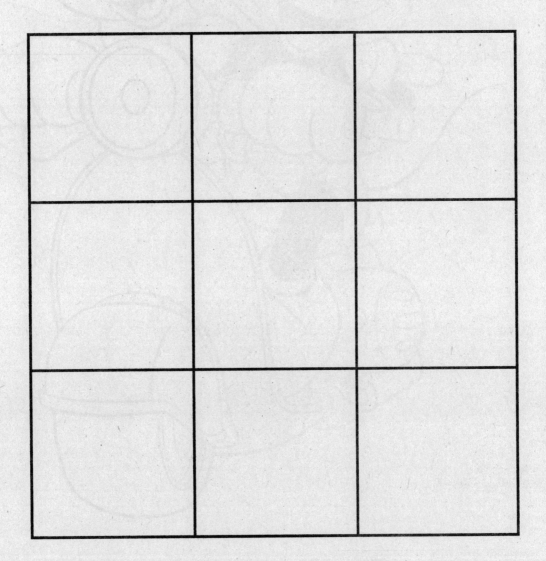

Time for an adventure!

Mickey and Minnie pal around all day.
Draw pictures of their silly afternoon.

at the park . . .

eating a snack . . .

© Disney

I'm ready to roll!

Where shall we go?

What is Minnie
thinking of?

SHOPPING SPREE!

You've won a shopping spree at your favorite store. Draw some cool things you would buy.

Minnie writes and draws
in her diary every day.
What would you draw
in your diary?

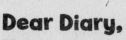

Dear Diary,
This is what I did today.

Minnie likes cheering for her friends. Create a cheer for Minnie, and have someone write it here.

_____

_____

_____

_____

_____

_____

_____

FAVORITE FRIENDS

Minnie and Daisy are the best of friends.
Draw one of your best friends.

My friend's name is: _____

MIRROR, MIRROR
Draw a self-portrait.

"Butterflies look like bows!"

Minnie loves butterflies.
Draw and color a beautiful butterfly!

Friendship warms the heart.

Say, cheese.

What a special way . . .

. . . to spend the day!

Circle 3 pictures of
flowers and 4 suns.

Fun in the sun!

Puppy Love

Sweetheart Minnie

Please come in!

Minnie's Bow-tique!

Decode the sign by matching letters to the shapes.

A B _ W   F _ R
♡   ♡

_ V _ RY
⋈ ⋈

_ _ A _ _ N!
⬡ ⋈ ⬡ ♡

Use this key to decode the sign.
⋈ =E   ⬡ =S   ♡ =O

So many to pick from!

It's bow-making time

Cuckoo-Loca

Figaro wants to help.

Good Friends

Let's make some bows!

Little Helpers

Helping Hands

What fun!

Making mischief!

Oops!

A splash of color!

Helpful Friends

Minnie's newest bows!

How many bow ties do you count?

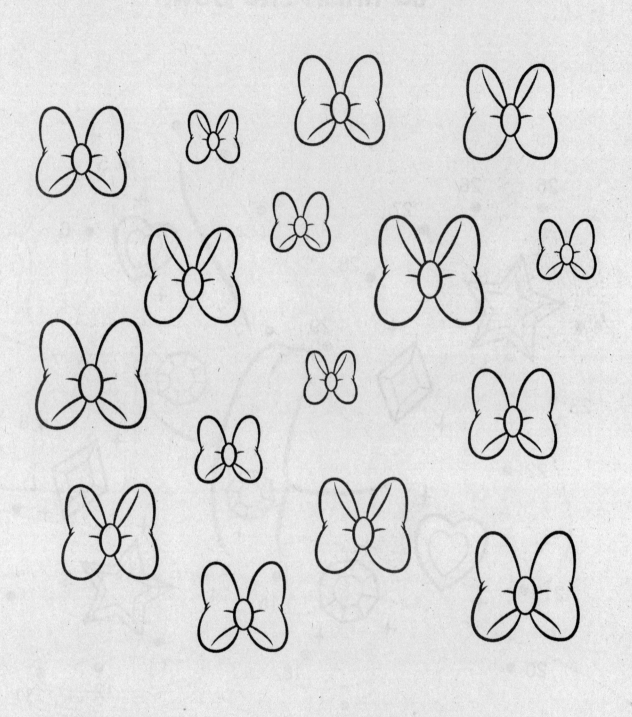

Your Answer: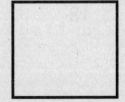

Connect the dots
to finish the bow.

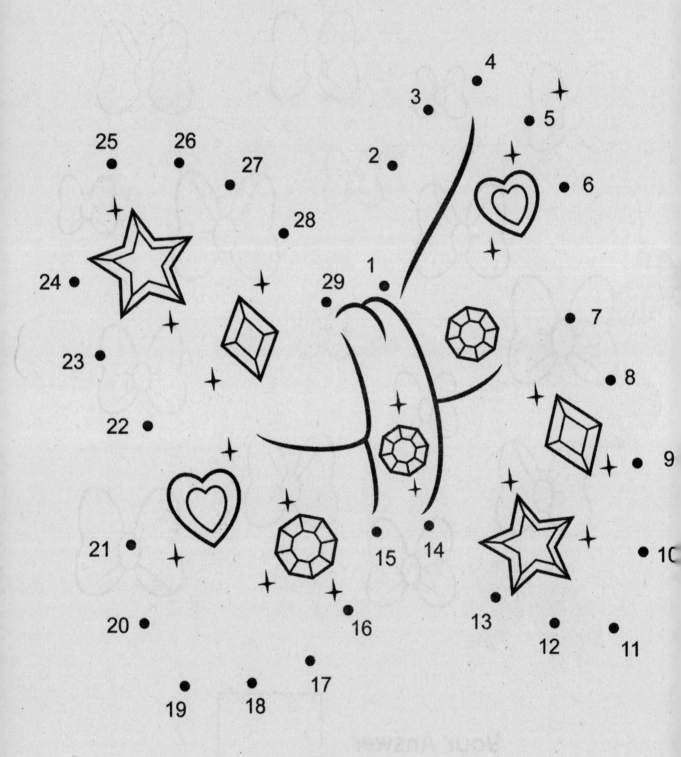

Superstar Penelope Poodle!

Going to the Dance!

Unscramble the words.

SOWB _ _ _ _

NEINMI _ _ _ _ _ _

RNOBIB _ _ _ _ _ _

SAYID _ _ _ _ _

EDASB _ _ _ _ _

© Disney

Balloon bow tie!

Goofy's Bow

Looking good!

Busy Day

There's no business like bow business!

Bows are Minnie's favorite accessory!
Color the bows.

Working Together

Leaky pipes!

© Disney

Follow the leaky pipes
to Clarabelle.

Start

Finish

Clarabelle sure is handy!

Help Daisy
with her drawing.

Oops! It's bathtime!

What numbers come next in the patterns?

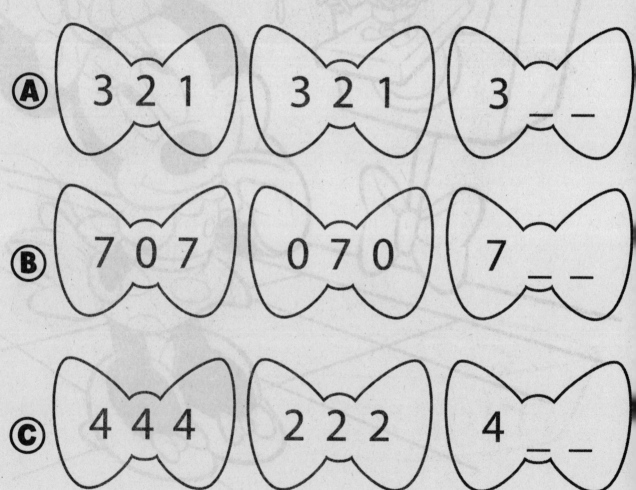

A) 3 2 1   3 2 1   3 _ _

B) 7 0 7   0 7 0   7 _ _

C) 4 4 4   2 2 2   4 _ _

Suppertime!

Matching cuteness!

Smile!

Which Minnie is different?

What does Figaro see?
Connect the dots to find out!

Wake up, Donald...

... It's time for breakfast!

© Disney

Better Together

Find and circle the words listed below.

FALL   **LEAF**
FIGARO **HEARTS**
BOW

```
F I G A R O O
A G B A C B
L B R B O W
L E A F A E
L S P D Q K
H E A R T S
```

Be happy!!

Match Minnie to her shadow.

Friends and fun forever!

Lambie is Doc's BFF.

Hallie is the receptionist at Doc's clinic.

© Disney

Stuffy the stuffed dragon is sometimes clumsy.

Chilly is Doc's favorite stuffed snowman.

© Disney

Doc and Donny are playing with their
stuffed animals. "Roar!" says Bronty.

"Ah!" says Doc. "Run away, Stuffy!"

© Disney

"Doc! Donny!" calls Dad. "Time for lunch."

"My salami sandwich is great, Dad," says Donny.

"Here, Bronty," says Donny. **"Have some salami!"**

**"Finish up, Donny," says Mom.
"I'll take you to soccer practice."**

© Disney

Circle the items that begin with the letter B.

"We'll be in the backyard, Dad!" says Doc.

© Disney

"This is fun," says Lambie. "Let's go, Bronty!"

"Hey, Lenny," says Bronty.

"Sorry," says Lenny. "I have to go!"

"I wonder why Lenny ran away," says Lambie.

© Disney

"I don't know!" says Bronty, breathing on Lambie.

"Bronty, your breath is smelly!" says Lambie.

"Time for a checkup!" says Doc.

"But I feel fine," says Bronty.

"You have bad breath, Bronty," says Hallie.

"I'm going to give you a dental checkup,"
says Doc.

© Disney

"Open wide!"

How many teeth does Bronty have?
Write your answer below.

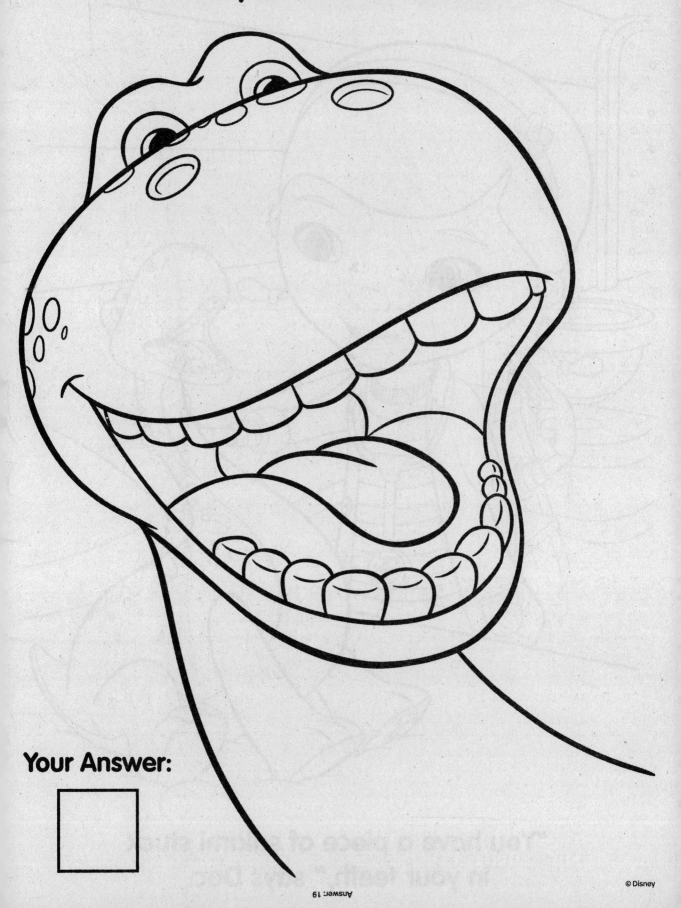

Your Answer:

© Disney

"You have a piece of salami stuck in your teeth," says Doc.

"You have Stinkysalamibreath!" says Doc.

© Disney

"Let's add that to the Big Book of Boo-Boos!"

"We can treat this with a toothbrush and toothpaste!"

© Disney

"Your breath is minty-fresh, Bronty!" says Lenny.
"Let's play!"

"Thanks, Doc!"

© Disney

Boo-boos be gone!

Doc and her friend Henry are ready to watch a meteor shower.

© Disney

"Anyone want a star cookie?" asks Dad.

Henry has a new telescope.

© Disney

"What do you see?" asks Doc. "A star?
Two stars? A whole galaxy?"

© Disney

**"I can't see a thing!" says Henry.
"Everything is fuzzy."**

"I'll see if I can fix it," says Doc.

"Better hurry," says Dad.
"The meteor shower will start soon!"

© Disney

**"Hi, Hallie," says Doc.
"Meet Aurora, our new patient!"**

© Disney

"This place is great," says Aurora.

© Disney

"Oh, sorry!" says Aurora. "Didn't see you there."

"Nice doggie!" says Aurora.

© Disney

"You need an eye exam," says Doc.

"Tell me what you see on this eye chart,"
says Doc.

© Disney

"Pretzels!" says Aurora.

Find all the monkeys.
How many do you count?

Your Answer:

© Disney

**"I have a diagnosis!" shouts Doc.
"Aurora has Blurrystaritis!"**

"Can you help her see better?" asks Lambie.

© Disney

"Doctors give kids—and hippos—glasses to help them see," says Doc.

© Disney

"I'll say!"

Find all the pictures of Aurora.
How many do you count?

Your Answer:

**"I think I see the problem!" says Doc.
"Your eyepiece is missing!"**

© Disney

"I wonder what happened to it," says Lambie.

© Disney

"Here it is!" says Stuffy. **"I found it!"**

© Disney

"This eyepiece will help you see clearly," says Doc.

© Disney

Draw what Henry wants to see through the telescope.

"Everything is so clear!" says Aurora. **"And close!"**

"I fixed the telescope!" says Doc.
"Just in time!" says Dad.

**"The meteor shower is happening!"
shouts Henry. "Thanks, Doc!"**

Welcome to the family, Sofia!

Princess Amber and Prince James are twins.

All hail Princess Sofia!

Which picture of Sofia is different?

Answer: B

The king gives Sofia the Amulet of Avalor.
She promises to always wear it!

© Disney

Princess Sofia wakes up.

© Disney

Time to get dressed.

© Disney

Time for school.

The Royal Coach

Connect the dots to complete the flying horse.

Welcome to Royal Prep—the Royal Preparatory Academy.

Headmistresses Flora, Fauna, and Merryweather

© Disney

Amber's best friends—Clio and Hildegard

© Disney

Unscramble the names!

O F A S I

_ _ _ _ _

E M R B A

_ _ _ _ _

O L I C

_ _ _ _

M E S A J

_ _ _ _ _

© Disney

Hurry to class.

Every princess must know how to curtsy.

Arts & Crafts

Draw what Sofia is painting.

Sofia makes new friends at Royal Prep.

Professor Popov's Dance Class

Recess!

© Disney

Put the pictures in order by numbering them 1-4.

A

B

C

D

_____

_____

_____

_____

© Disney

Amber and Clio share a secret.

Hildegard gets an "A" in Fan Fluttering.

© Disney

Time to Study

© Disney

Find and circle 4 pictures of Sofia and 3 books.

Be careful, Sofia!

Magic Class

Learning to be a princess is not easy!

Home Sweet Home

Find and circle 7 items that begin with the letter B.

A Royal Tea Party

Oops!

Amber wonders if Sofia will ever be a real princess.

Match the shadows to their owners.

© Disney

Baileywick announces that dinner is served.

© Disney

Sofia has so much to learn!

© Disney

Count the tableware.

How many forks do you see?

How many knives do you see?

How many spoons do you see?

Add all the silverware together.

"How was your day, dear?"

Sofia misses her village friends.

Ruby and Jade

A Royal Sleepover

There are 6 differences between the two pictures. Can you find them?

A Royal Makeover

Best Friends Forever!

Homework with Vivian—Build a Dream Castle

Draw your own Dream Castle.

Sofia and Clover

Robin and Mia

Whatnaught

Hide and Seek
Find and circle the 10 animals.

The Flying Derby is about to begin.

Sofia and Minimus

Prince Hugo bumps into Sofia!

Help Sofia and Minimus win the race!

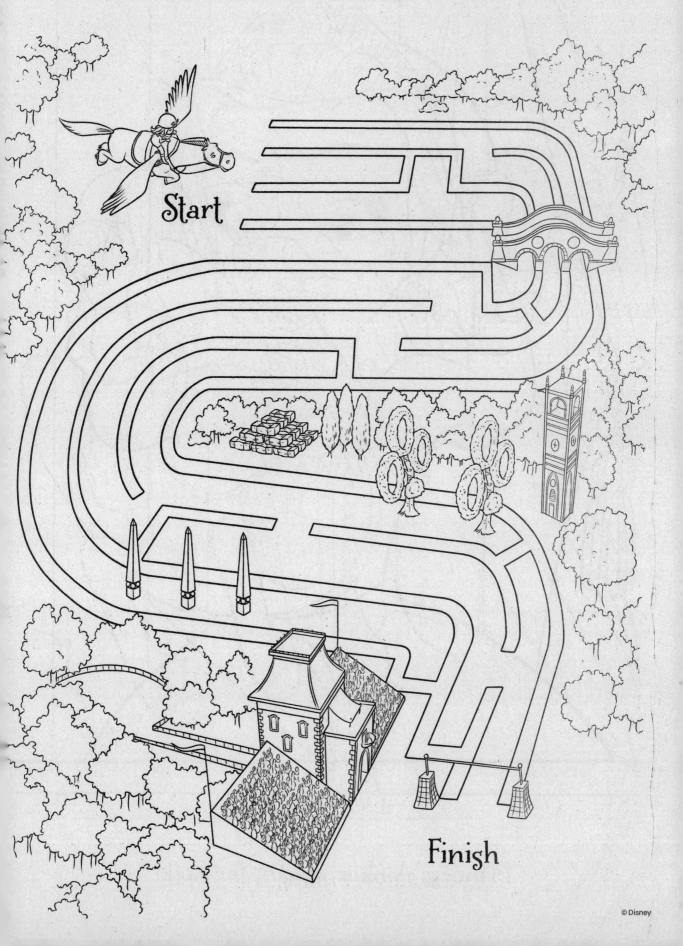

Start

Finish

Princess Amber cheers for Sofia.

Sofia wins!

Count the flying horses!

Answer: 14

The Royal Family Portrait

Hooray for Princess Sofia the First!